I Oshiyah Div.5

The Sorcerer's Apprentice

retold for easy reading
by ANNE McKIE

illustrated by KEN McKIE

Ladybird Books

This strange story began many years ago in a country far away, where a small valley lay at the foot of a high mountain. The people who lived in the valley often looked up at the mountain. Sometimes through a break in the clouds they could see a huge castle with high walls and dark towers. No one from the valley had ever entered the castle, or had even climbed the steep path up the mountain.

Once, the valley had been a wonderful place to live. Everyone was happy and no one ever went hungry. They all worked together in the fields which grew fine crops. The trees in the orchards were always heavy with fruit, and the vineyards grew huge juicy grapes for wine. All was peace and contentment.

Then one autumn a very strange thing happened. When the villagers went to gather in their harvest, all their fine crops had gone. Everything had disappeared. The trees were stripped bare of fruit and not one ear of corn was left anywhere.

"It must have happened during the night," cried one angry farmer.

"Some wicked thieves have taken the lot," yelled another, waving his stick furiously. "Just wait till I catch up with them!"

For weeks the villagers tried to find the thieves. They looked for clues — footprints on the ground — a trail of grain — but they found nothing. It was as if someone had waved a magic wand and made the whole harvest vanish.

That winter the people lived on the food they had wisely stored in their barns from other years.

The following spring they planted their crops once again. Autumn came and the harvest was even bigger and better than before. Every night the men stood guard in the fields and orchards. They were taking no chances this time.

But one dreadful morning the village awoke to find everything had gone again, just the same as the year before.

"It must be magic!" cried the people in fear. "This valley is bewitched!" Some of the younger children began to cry.

"We will all starve this winter," sobbed one old lady. "What can we do? Who will help us?"

Suddenly a young lad called Jim stepped forward. "Let me solve the mystery and seek my fortune at the same time," he pleaded. "I am very strong — and quite clever sometimes," he said jokingly. And before anyone could stop him, he ran out of the village square, and was quickly out of sight up the mountain.

Soon young Jim had left his sunny valley far behind. The mountain mist began to swirl around him, but he was not afraid. He stopped to cut himself a walking stick from a small tree growing on the track. As he climbed on, he whistled and sang cheerfully.

"I should get to the top very soon," Jim panted out loud.

"You are there, young fellow," a deep voice boomed. And out of the shadows stepped a strange old man.

Jim gasped. He had never before seen a man dressed in such unusual clothes. His hood and robes were dark and flowing. They were decorated with jewels and threads which flashed and sparkled in weird patterns. In one hand he held a wand, and on his wrist perched a big black raven. "He must be a great magician or a famous sorcerer," thought Jim to himself, his heart pounding.

"Night is falling and my castle is very near," said the Sorcerer, beckoning to the boy. "Come and spend the night with me."

Jim followed him, and soon they were right inside the walls of the castle.

As the Sorcerer strode across the courtyard, Jim noticed great piles of food stacked all around. Suddenly the black raven flew down and

14

perched on Jim's shoulder. "That's the harvest from your valley," he croaked. "He steals it every year for himself."

"I'll kill him!" cried young Jim. "Leaving our people to starve like that!"

"Don't be stupid. He can kill you with one glance," screeched the bird. "Take my advice. Stay here and learn his secrets, and then you can defeat his evil spells."

15

All at once the Sorcerer turned round. "Are you looking for work?" he demanded. "Because if you are, I need an apprentice."

Jim quickly agreed to become his servant in return for lessons in magic. That way he was sure he could bring back happiness to the valley below.

The castle was enormous, and full of treasures and precious things. The Sorcerer took Jim from room to room, each one better than the one before. At last they came to the Great Hall. It was so big that Jim could hardly see the other side. Tapestries hung from the ceiling and suits of armour lined the walls. Jim walked slowly across the huge room.

"This is where the Sorcerer works his magic," he thought to himself, excitedly.

The shelves were full of ancient books, some too heavy for Jim to lift. Enormous bottles of vivid coloured liquids bubbled and hissed in one corner. Right in the middle of the Hall sat a great black cauldron almost as tall as Jim. "As my apprentice, you must keep my cauldron filled to

the brim. And woe betide you if I find it empty!'' the Sorcerer said, frowning.

''I'll start work right away,'' said Jim, eagerly.

''When all your tasks are finished, I will teach you my magic,'' promised the Sorcerer.

So Jim became the Sorcerer's apprentice. Day after day the work became harder and harder, and the hours longer. But still Jim learned no magic.

During the weeks that followed, the Sorcerer's raven became Jim's friend. For many years he had been under a spell cast by the Sorcerer. He

could fly quite freely around the castle, but as soon as he wanted to glide down to the valley below, his wings just folded up and he had to land. "Will you take me with you when you escape from here?" he asked Jim.

"I'm not a prisoner," laughed Jim. "I can walk out now and go home." With that, he picked up the raven and marched out of the castle gate.

All of a sudden he stopped dead. No matter how hard he tried, he couldn't move one step forward.

"Now do you believe me?" croaked the bird. "We are both the Sorcerer's prisoners."

When Jim realised that the Sorcerer had cast a spell on him too, he became even more determined to outwit his master.

The Sorcerer seemed to know this, and worked his apprentice even harder than before. All day long he stirred up great bowls full of magic potions. Some of them smelled terrible! Jim had to carry great books of spells around until his arms ached. But the worst task of all was keeping the great black cauldron filled to the brim.

The stream from which Jim had to bring the water was far away from the Great Hall, down flights of stone steps, across cobbled yards and deep in the castle grounds. Jim had to make trip after trip with two heavy buckets full of water. "If only I knew some magic words," he sighed, "I could make these buckets fly on their own."

"If you knew any magic words at all,"
grumbled the raven crossly, "you could get us
both out of here." The bird went on, "Haven't
you ever realised, my lad, that the Sorcerer never
lets you hear one word he says, when he is casting
his spells."

"You're right!" gasped Jim. "All we've got to do is to overhear the magic words and we'll be free."

This was easier said than done. Jim and the raven tried everything. They crept up behind the Sorcerer in total silence. They hid behind his treasure chest. They crouched under his table. They even tried asking him. This made the old man even more suspicious than before. Not only did he work Jim hard all day, but late into the night, too.

One night Jim was too tired to climb up the
stairs to his room at the top of the castle. It was
so late that he fell fast asleep in a dark corner
behind the Sorcerer's chair. The old man did not
see him, because he was far too busy with his
spells. Then by accident, he knocked one of his
glass bottles off the table. It fell to the floor and
smashed into pieces.

The sound of the crash woke Jim up straightaway, and he stared in astonishment as the Sorcerer beckoned to a broom next to him. Loudly the Sorcerer uttered the MAGIC WORDS.

Jim watched in wonder as the broom danced across the room on its own. Quietly and neatly it swept up the broken glass, then ran back to its place next to Jim.

Still the Sorcerer had not noticed the boy in the dark corner. At last he left the room and went to bed.

It was long after midnight when Jim crept up the stairs, repeating the magic words to himself in delight.

He was awake before dawn, ready to begin a spell. The raven gave him a stern warning. "Take my advice. Wait until the Sorcerer has gone out — or you will be sorry."

After what seemed like hours, the old man left the castle. He left Jim the usual hard task of filling the big black cauldron. The raven flew up to the top of the castle and watched until the Sorcerer was out of sight.

Jim wasted no time. He uttered the magic words, then ordered the broom to fetch water.

Immediately the broom grew two long spindly arms and grabbed the buckets. It marched down the Great Hall, leapt down the steps and straight down to the stream. Jim and the raven followed in amazement.

The broom was so quick that the cauldron was soon full to the brim. But it went on fetching bucket after bucket full of water. Soon water was flooding all over the Hall floor.

"Quick!" screeched the raven. "Stop it. Stop it at once."

"I can't, I can't!" screamed Jim. "I don't know the magic words to *stop* spells."

The broom kept on working. More and more water was poured into the cauldron.

Now the whole room was flooded, and books and papers floated on the rising water. Tables and chairs bobbed about as the water swirled round the room.

In desperation, Jim grabbed an axe and split the broom down the middle. To his horror, the two halves picked up extra buckets — and *both* began to fetch more water.

Soon not only was the Great Hall flooded, but water swept down the stairs and through the castle and courtyard.

All at once, the sky grew dark and there was a noise like thunder. A great shadow fell across Jim and the raven.

The Sorcerer had returned. His towering rage was like a storm. His anger lit up the Great Hall like lightning. He screamed the magic words to stop the broom and an icy wind swept through the room.

At once everything was back to normal.

Very slowly, a smile spread across Jim's face. For in his rage, the Sorcerer had uttered the

magic words that stop all spells. Jim had heard them at last.

"Beat him! Beat him!" cried the furious old man to the broom. Just as the broom was about to crack down on Jim's shoulders, the boy shouted the magic words he had just learned. Back to the corner went the broom.

"Now I know the words to start spells, and to stop them," cried Jim in glee, "and you told me them yourself, Sorcerer. You're finished at last." Jim danced round the old wizard in delight. "Your wicked spells are at an end for ever."

The raven flew up into the beams of the roof in fear.

The Sorcerer smiled an evil smile. He
beckoned Jim towards him. He bent his head
very close to the boy and whispered in his ear.
"Of course you have learned my secrets, you
clever boy. You're the best apprentice I have ever
had," the Sorcerer went on.

Jim was surprised. Perhaps the old man was
sorry for his evil ways.

"Beware the Sorcerer, beware, beware!"
screeched the raven from the roof.

In a blinding flash the Sorcerer changed into a huge snarling bear. With one swipe of his great paw he knocked Jim to the ground.

As the bear chased him everywhere, Jim tried to hide behind the Sorcerer's chair. But the bear smashed it to splinters with one blow.

Soon Jim was trapped in a corner. The raven flew down as low as he dared. "Change yourself into a snake, bears hate snakes," he cawed.

Jim had quite forgotten that he had the same magic powers as the Sorcerer.

One wish and Jim became a snake, slithering towards the bear. Another flash and the bear changed into an eagle. The snake drew back, but the eagle grabbed him by the tail with his sharp talons.

"Change again, change again," croaked the raven once more.

Jim had hardly time to think as he became a wildcat, spitting and snarling.

He sprang at the eagle, but the eagle was too quick to be caught. He spread his wings and rose into the air. The wildcat just managed to grab a couple of his giant tail feathers.

The startled eagle flew out of the Great Hall, through the castle and into the grounds. The wildcat sped after him, quick as lightning.

The eagle reached the stream where Jim drew water to fill up the black cauldron, then suddenly he vanished.

The wildcat crouched by the stream and peered into the water. Where was the Sorcerer?

A small silver fish swam to the surface, and a voice spoke. "I have defeated you, you stupid apprentice. My magic is far greater than yours!" It was the Sorcerer changed into a fish.

"I'll change back into a boy, and wade into the stream and catch him," whispered Jim to the raven.

"Be cunning!" croaked the bird, from the bank. Then he flew across and whispered in Jim's ear.

"Sorcerer," shouted Jim to the fish, "prove how great you are, and change yourself into anything I choose!"

"I will show you how great I am!" The castle shook, so loud was the voice of the Sorcerer. "From this tiny fish, I will become a mountain!" boasted the old man.

"Oh no," replied Jim. "Change yourself into something small. That's much more difficult, Sorcerer. Turn yourself into a drop of water."

Another blinding flash, and the Sorcerer's magic words echoed round the mountains.

Soon the great voice faded away to nothing. Everything was silent. The clear stream gurgled and sparkled, as it flowed out of the castle grounds. It splashed down the hillside into the river in the valley, and out into the open sea.

Jim and the raven hugged each other in glee. They danced on the bank of the little stream, and laughed and laughed.

"He's tricked himself," said Jim, quite breathless. "When he turned into a drop of water, he was swallowed up by the water of the stream. Soon he'll be lost in the ocean for ever."

Jim and the raven rolled on the grass in delight at the thought. "He's gone for ever," chuckled the raven. "We're free at last."

Without even one look back at the castle, Jim and the raven went down the mountain path.

What a welcome awaited them in the valley! What stories were told of their adventures!

Jim still had his magic power, and soon he brought back happiness to his valley. "I promise to always use my magic for good and never for evil," he said with a smile.

"And I shall make sure that you do," croaked his friend the raven.